This book belongs

to Salina Dublin

"Christening" April 26, 1987

ISBN 0 86163 083 1

© Award Publications Limited 1982
Spring House, Spring Place
Kentish Town London NW5, 3BH, England

Printed in Belgium

MORE
BRER RABBIT
STORIES

Illustrated by

RENE CLOKE

AWARD PUBLICATIONS — LONDON

BRER RABBIT AND BRER FOX

Brer Rabbit was a naughty little fellow.
He liked to play tricks on Brer Fox,
Brer Wolf and the other animals who were
always trying to catch him.

But Brer Rabbit was so clever that he
managed to escape every time and went on
playing his tricks.

One day, Brer Wolf and Brer Fox
decided to put a stop to this so
they made a plan.

"I've thought of a good idea,"
said Brer Wolf, "run home and get
into bed and pretend to be dead
and I will go to Brer Rabbit's
house with the news. When Brer Rabbit
comes to look at you, just jump up and
catch him!"

"That should be easy," agreed
Brer Fox and he trotted home
and went to bed.

As soon as Brer Fox had gone, Brer Wolf went along to Brer Rabbit's house and called out —

"Are you there, Brer Rabbit? Sad news, poor Brer Fox died this morning. I'm just going around to tell his friends," and off he ran.

When the wolf had gone, Brer Rabbit sat down and thought hard.

"This sounds like a trick," he said and decided to go to Brer Fox's house and see for himself if the fox was really dead.

When he got to Brer Fox's house, he walked carefully around to see if any traps were set and then he peeped into the window.

There was Brer Fox, lying on the bed, with his eyes shut so Brer Rabbit went to the open door.

"Poor Brer Fox," he said aloud, "I wonder if he is really dead? I think he must be for he lies very still; I had better wait here until his friends come."

Then he had another look at Brer Fox.
"You can always tell when a fox is dead," he said, "because he keeps shaking his left leg."

When Brer Fox heard this, he thought he had better shake his leg but, of course, as soon as he did this, Brer Rabbit knew that he was just pretending.

He dashed out of the house and didn't stop running until he was safely home.

"They can't catch me with that trick," he laughed.

And he went on laughing all the time he was having his tea.

THE TAR-BABY

Brer Fox tried to think of a good way to catch Brer Rabbit but the rabbit was always too clever for him.

One day, Brer Fox worked out a new plan.

With a lot of tar he made a tar-baby, put a hat on its head and stuck it on a stick near Brer Rabbit's house; then he hid in some bushes and waited to see what would happen.

Before long, Brer Rabbit came walking by and, when he saw the tar-baby, he stopped and looked at it in surprise; he had never seen anything quite like that before.

"Good-morning," said Brer Rabbit, "it's a fine day."

But the tar-baby didn't answer.

"Can't you hear me?" shouted Brer Rabbit at the top of his voice.

But still the tar-baby didn't answer.

This made Brer Rabbit so angry that he rushed up and hit the tar-baby and, of course, his paw stuck to the tar.

"Let go" yelled Brer Rabbit, "or I'll hit you again!"

So he hit out with his other paws and those stuck as well.

There was Brer Rabbit stuck to the tar-baby and he couldn't get off.

Then Brer Fox walked out from the bushes and laughed, for this was just what he had hoped would happen.

"You seem to be stuck up this morning, Brer Rabbit" he said, "now I've caught you at last and I mean to punish you.

You won't play any more tricks on me!"

Brer Rabbit thought quickly.

"Do what you like with me, Brer Fox," he cried, "but don't throw me into the briar patch!

Hang me or drown me but, *please*, don't throw me into the briar patch!"

"That must be the best way to hurt him," thought Brer Fox, so he pulled Brer Rabbit from the tar-baby and flung him into the briar patch.

"That will be the end of him!" he barked.

But, in a moment, Brer Rabbit had scrambled out.

"I was born and bred in a briar patch!" he laughed as he scampered home, "born and bred in a briar patch!"

BRER RABBIT AND BRER TORTOISE

When Brer Rabbit was out one day, he saw Brer Fox hustling along with a sack over his shoulder; he seemed to be in a great hurry.

Something was kicking and shouting inside the sack.

"That sounds like someone I know," said Brer Rabbit, "I believe it's Brer Tortoise"

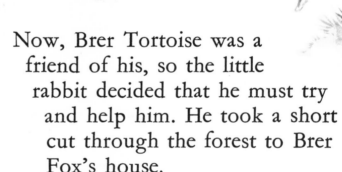

Now, Brer Tortoise was a friend of his, so the little rabbit decided that he must try and help him. He took a short cut through the forest to Brer Fox's house.

When he got there, he ran into the garden and tore up a lot of plants from the flower beds.

Then he hid by the front door.

After a time, Brer Fox appeared with the sack over his shoulder and Brer Rabbit called out —

"Fetch a big stick, Brer Fox! Someone is tearing up plants in your garden!"

Dropping the sack on the doorstep, Brer Fox took up a stick and rushed into the garden.

While he was searching for the rascal, Brer Rabbit undid the sack and let out his friend Brer Tortoise.

Then, between them, they took one of Brer Fox's beehives and stuffed it into the sack.

"That will give him a surprise!" whispered Brer Rabbit as they tied up the sack and put it back on the doorstep.

Brer Fox came back from the garden feeling very angry because he couldn't find anyone pulling up his plants. He picked up the sack and went into his house, slamming the door behind him.

Brer Rabbit and Brer Tortoise sat in the bushes and waited.

Then they heard a great noise of buzzing and yelping, and out ran Brer Fox with the angry bees buzzing around him and stinging him as he ran.

"I thought I had captured a tortoise in my sack!" howled Brer Fox, "how can I have made such a mistake?"

"Ha, ha!" laughed Brer Rabbit, "that will teach him to leave tortoises alone — they might turn into a hive of bees!"
The two friends hurried off before Brer Fox discovered that they had tricked him.

BRER RABBIT AND BRER FOX GO FISHING

On a very hot day, all the animals were digging a patch of ground together so that they could plant some vegetables.

As Brer Rabbit was rather small, he found it hard work and after a time he threw down his fork and called out —

"I've got a thorn in my paw, I must stop and pull it out."

He walked off to a shady spot and pretended to get the thorn from his paw. Then he saw, a little way off, a well with a bucket hanging from it. "How cool that looks!" thought Brer Rabbit, "I'll hop into that bucket and have a nap."

But as soon as he stepped into the bucket,
it started going down the well.

"Ho! ho!" gasped Brer Rabbit, "where am
I going?"

Down, down went the bucket; the well was dark and cold and
when, at last, the bucket hit the water the rabbit, very frightened,
wondered what to do next.

Brer Fox had been watching Brer Rabbit and, thinking he was up
to a trick, he followed him into the wood. He saw him jump into
the bucket and disappear.

"That's a funny thing to do," he muttered, "I wonder if Brer Rabbit keeps all his money down there?"

He peeped into the well and saw Brer Rabbit sitting in the bucket in the water.

"What are you doing down there?" he called to him.

"Oh, I'm fishing," replied Brer Rabbit, "I thought some fish would be a nice surprise for dinner for us all."

"Are there many down there?" asked Brer Fox, peering into the well.

"Oh, yes! Dozens and dozens of them!" answered Brer Rabbit, "come and help me and we'll soon have enough for everyone."

"How can I get down?" the fox asked him.

"Just get into the other bucket," said Brer Rabbit, "that will bring you down."

Brer Rabbit seemed to be having a very good time and, as Brer Fox was fond of fish, he decided to join him.

Although he was rather big for the bucket, he managed to creep into it.

But, of course, he was much heavier than the little rabbit and, as his bucket went down, Brer Rabbit's bucket came up.

"Catch a nice bucketful of fish, Brer Fox!" cried Brer Rabbit as the buckets passed each other, "it's nice and cool down there!"

It was a long time before someone helped Brer Fox out of the well and, by that time, Brer Rabbit had run home.